Put Beginning Readers on the Right Track with
ALL ABOARD READING™

The All Aboard Reading series is especially for beginning readers. Written by noted authors and illustrated in full color, these are books that children really and truly *want* to read—books to excite their imagination, tickle their funny bone, expand their interests, and support their feelings. With four different reading levels, All Aboard Reading lets you choose which books are most appropriate for your children and their growing abilities.

Picture Readers—for Ages 3 to 6
Picture Readers have super-simple texts with many nouns appearing as rebus pictures. At the end of each book are 24 flash cards—on one side is the rebus picture; on the other side is the written-out word.

Level 1—for Preschool through First Grade Children
Level 1 books have very few lines per page, very large type, easy words, lots of repetition, and pictures with visual "cues" to help children figure out the words on the page.

Level 2—for First Grade to Third Grade Children
Level 2 books are printed in slightly smaller type than Level 1 books. The stories are more complex, but there is still lots of repetition in the text and many pictures. The sentences are quite simple and are broken up into short lines to make reading easier.

Level 3—for Second Grade through Third Grade Children
Level 3 books have considerably longer texts, use harder words and more complicated sentences.

All Aboard for happy reading!

For J, N, & K, of course — R.A.H.

For my daughter Paris and
my friend Ronnie — B.O.

Library of Congress Cataloging-in-Publication Data

Herman, Ronnie Ann.
    Pal the pony / by Ronnie Ann Herman ; illustrated by Betina Ogden.
       p.   cm. — (All aboard reading)
    Summary: Pal the pony is too little to participate in the rodeo but becomes the star of the ranch in a different way.
    1. Ponies—Juvenile fiction. [1. Ponies—Fiction. 2. Ranch life—Fiction. 3. Rodeos—Fiction. 4. Size—Fiction.] I. Ogden, Betina, ill. II. Title. III. Series.
PZ10.3.H465Pal   1996
[E]—dc20

95-30265
CIP
AC

ISBN 0-448-41257-8   D E F G H I J

Preschool-Grade 1

PAL THE PONY

By R. A. Herman
Illustrated by Betina Ogden

Grosset & Dunlap • New York

Pal is a little pony.

He lives on the Star Ranch.

Today is a big day.

It is rodeo time.

All the cowboys and horses
get ready.

Blaze runs all around
the ranch.

She wants to be
the fastest horse
at the rodeo.

Pal tries to run fast, too.

But his legs are too short.

Samson pulls and pulls.
He will pull the big wagon
for the hay ride.

Pal tries to pull, too.

But he is not very strong.

Kicker kicks and bucks.

He is the best bucking bronco.

Pal tries to kick
and buck, too.

Oops! Down he goes.

Poor Pal.
He is too little
for the rodeo.

So he just nibbles some grass
and swishes his tail.

Nibble, nibble.

Swish, swish.

A little girl sees Pal.

"What a cute pony," she says.

"Do you want to ride him?"

asks a cowboy.

"Yes!" says the girl.
So—trot, trot, trot—
off they go.

They go past the barn,

past the pond,

and—trot, trot, trot—
back again.

The little girl hugs Pal.
She gives him an apple.

"You are my pal,"

she says.

Now all the children
want a ride.

Pal does not run
or pull or kick.
Even the littlest child
can ride Pal.

Pal is the littlest pony
on the Star Ranch.
But Pal is the biggest star
of all!